*These Possible Lives*

Fleur Jaeggy

# THESE
# POSSIBLE LIVES

*Translated by Minna Zallman Proctor*

A NEW DIRECTIONS BOOK

Published by arrangement with Adelphi Edizioni, Milan.

New Directions gratefully acknowledges the support of Pro Helvetia, Swiss Arts Council.

swiss arts council

## pro:helvetia

First published as a New Directions Paperbook Original in 2017
Manufactured in the United States of America
Design by Erik Rieselbach

*Library of Congress Cataloging-in-Publication Data*
Names: Jaeggy, Fleur, author. | Proctor, Minna, translator.
Title: These possible lives / Fleur Jaeggy ; translated by Minna Zallman Proctor.
Other titles: Vite congetturali. English
Description: First American paperback edition. | New York : New Directions, 2017.
Identifiers: LCCN 2017000507 | ISBN 9780811226875 (acid-free paper)
Subjects: LCSH: De Quincey, Thomas, 1785–1859. | Keats, John, 1795–1821. | Schwob, Marcel, 1867–1905.
Classification: LCC PQ4870.A4 V5813 2017 | DDC 854/.914 [B] —dc23
LC record available at https://lccn.loc.gov/2017000507

10 9 8 7 6 5

New Directions Books are published for James Laughlin
by New Directions Publishing Corporation
80 Eighth Avenue, New York 10011

# Contents

*Thomas De Quincey*

Thomas De Quincey became a visionary in 1791 when he was six years old. His older brother William was looking for a way to walk on the ceiling upside down like a fly. Richard, whom they called Pink, signed on to a whaling ship and was captured by pirates. The other siblings were depressives. Thomas leafed listlessly through the pages of *Aladdin and the Enchanted Lamp*. Every morning Mrs. De Quincey inspected the children, perfuming them with lavender or rose water, and then icily dismissed them from her presence until lunch. Dreams of "terrific grandeur" settled on the nursery. A *delectatio morosa* had clawed its way in; the children took on the peculiar appearance, malevolent and lucid, of those who frolic with nightmares—those who are *touched with pensiveness*—which Baudelaire then translated *marqué par la rêverie fatale.* His sister Jane lived three years. When she died, Thomas thought that she would come back, like a crocus. Children who grow up in the country know about death; they can, in a manner of speaking, see their own bones out the window, in the frugal garden plots. Thomas planted an herb garden and when he finished, he solemnly stopped waiting for Jane. Observing the winter garden, the remnants of vegetation poking out through the snow, their slow dialogue with their own brittle roots, he deplored "that disgusting thing that is the degeneration of the winter approaching spring." From the first week in November until the end of January he pleaded with the sky: he wanted more snow, more ice, more storms and frost. His sister Elizabeth fell sick and Thomas fancied he saw a "*tiara* of light or a gleaming *aureola*," a sign of her "premature intellectual grandeur." Mr. Percival— friend of the Marquis de Condorecet and Jean-Baptiste le Rond d'Alembert as well as Mr. Charles White; noted for his paper on human craniology proposing the measurement of heads selected from all varieties of the human species—was summoned. The cause of death was *Hydrocephalus*. Thomas put forth a different theory: not that the sickness would have stimulated the "preternatural growth of the intellect," but rather the inverse, arguing that "this growth of the intellect coming on spontaneously" had outrun the capacities of physical structure. Old age descended on the child. Thomas took his leave of youth, like a caliph takes leave of his rosebush. Sneaking over to Elizabeth, the desolate *dandy* stared at her transparent eyelids. He noted the Bible and other small objects in the dim room, and then heard a cracking sound, hollow and desolate— everything had become so remote. A requiem shone between the girl's stiffening hands, the light was mocking and complicit. The boy set about writing. He dictated his memories to the airless quiet, to the ashes, to destiny's whispering ways, that gloomy exclamation point, the visions, the apathy. He wished for long life. He gathered up his gloves, hat, and white handkerchief, and headed off to the funeral procession, quoting "sweet and solemn farewell" as he went.

His father, owner of Quincey and Duck Linen Drapers, Manchester, lived in Lisbon, the Portuguese mountains, and in St. Kitts in the West Indies—all in the hope of forestalling the deterioration of his lungs. Then he'd come home and languish on a divan for weeks at a time. Words sprang to life, like "execution," "legacy," and "guardians," of which Thomas had four: a banker, a merchant, a judge, and the Reverend Samuel Hall. The child, observing like a mere bystander, shudders gently. He listened to three hundred sermons by Reverend Hall and was assigned to write summaries from memory. At the Grammar School of Bath he was subject to corporal punishment if he made mistakes. A blow to the head from a teacher's ruler. In those days, at certain charity schools, students were actually tortured. There were reports of one child who was branded with a hot iron. Sluggish and slow-witted from hunger, some were bedridden. Others were locked in basement cells. They didn't dare strike Charles Lamb, with his spindly legs. Coleridge wept, convinced he was going to die there. In Yorkshire, at Cowan Bridge, there was a school for the children of clergy. The children were toughened up—it was their directive—learning how to maintain a gelid expression and never reveal pain. They ate burned porridge. Maria and Elizabeth Brontë died after just a few months. Charlotte and Emily returned to the parsonage in Haworth only after the school was closed due to a typhoid epidemic, and went back to their needlepoint.

In the month of July, 1802, a trunk toppled down the stairs of the Grammar School of Manchester. It belonged to Thomas De Quincey and heralded the beginning of the tale of the teenage runaway. He would turn his back on the empty desks, the thought baubles that had been indulged there—he left them behind as if they were objects. The vestiges of his precocious erudition seemed to dissipate in the first light of dawn. He would no longer respond at roll call, and instead wandered nameless through the English countryside and the city of London. Umbrella in hand and the plays of Euripides in his pocket, he started walking. Thomas was on an adventure in poverty, relying on no resources beyond the tenuous protocol of frugality. In London he shared neither the gruel of the poor nor the crumbs of the wealthy, feeding instead on the hand-me-downs of a moneylender. Mr. Brunell liked the wan creature who'd descended on him like a stray—with his deliberate distractibility, his begging, and his theories about the price of furnished rooms, groceries, trout, butter, and onions. The cost of knowledge about the great world had exhausted TDQ. How much, he asked himself, could one day's happiness cost? Half a guinea? Rapacity was the moneylender's dominant frame of mind and although he was amicably disposed somewhere deep inside, or else gave the illusion of kindness, he didn't allow himself to be constrained by the formalities of his station or by any proclivity to compassion. He ate cookies while sitting on the only chair. The loan shark and the scholar, the latter always on his feet, spoke of Greek and Roman classics. The mice stopped short on their tear, discerning in the hungry yet trustworthy young client a new roommate for their sordid manor. They watched him grow agitated in his sleep, motoring his legs upward only to stop short intermittently, his gears slipping like a machine's. They heard him call out his own name, heard him moan and then cock his ear in the silence, listening for the sound to repeat. His voice, emerging from the ominous murk of dreams, passed alongside, fleeting like the miserable yelps of sleeping dogs.

Cloaked in a driver's mantle, some legal papers, and frost, Thomas surprised his shoes and went skating down the street, coasting to a stop on the corner of Oxford Street in front of his little friend Ann.

A pen-on-paper drawing of a London street, a

clock, an empty hourglass—the slightest geomantic sketch reveals the place where TDQ was introduced to opium. A weak smile crept upon his lips and he almost laughed aloud, as in a memory. It was perhaps a morning in March (or was it the autumn?) in 1804. His lapidary voice, incurably affable, pronounced high praise of the potion. His entry into that world was like being a guest in the pages of a richly illustrated encyclopedia for children, where inanimate objects have the sturdiness of intoxication momentarily evanesced. Happiness teased him, then tilted, almost as if happiness were itself in a rage—or some graceful convulsion of nature.

After reading Kant, he thought he might go live in a Canadian monastery. But was drawn instead to Dove Cottage, where Wordsworth had lived. The walls were hidden behind a dense fall of ivy; the façade was decorated with rose, jasmine, and honeysuckle. The friendship with Wordsworth deteriorated in time. The death of the poet's young daughter, Kate, should have brought the men together again, and yet that never happened. De Quincey knelt every night over the child's grave. He increased his dosage of laudanum. Wordsworth may well have found fault with the self-indulgent aspects of TDQ's grief, his demonstrable lack of faith in Providence. It was midnight, a few months later, when Thomas felt a singular sensation shooting from his knee down his calf. It lasted for five hours and when it was over, despair abdicated. He was overcome with laughter. The memory of Kate disappeared and her little red morocco shoes were deposited alongside other secular relics.

Henry Fuseli ate a diet of raw meat in order to obtain splendid dreams; Lamb spoke of "Lilliputian rabbits" when eating frog fricassee; and his sister Mary, wielding a knife, chased a little girl who was helping her in the kitchen and then stabbed her own mother through the heart; Hazlitt was perceptive about musculature and boxers; Wordsworth used a buttery knife to cut the pages of a first-edition Burke. Coleridge, his head shrouded in a fog, read poetry badly and moaned gloomily. The dreams of Jean Paul, the crow that loved the storm, reverberated across the Lake District. This was TDQ's Western Passage.

To the East: ibis and crocodiles found him pedantic — the flâneur was driven forward by opium-fueled theological caprices. A pack of gods clutched him. The pyramids, hospice of the dead. He dreamed up the abominable crocodile head and the turbaned Malay, delighting in the sickness and horror of original matter, deposits of which could be traced back to the stars.

There were others who helped themselves to dreams. Robert Southey experimented with laughing gas. Ann Radcliffe sought out huge quantities of indigestible food to reinforce her terrible night visions. Mrs. Leigh Hunt was proud to have produced an apocalyptic dream, which then appeared in a poem by Shelley. Coleridge, distracted by the scratching of his pen over the paper while transcribing his dream, forgot part of it. And Lamb complained about the derelict impoverishment of his dreams.

With gracious ceremony, Thomas addressed the staff in the kitchen. On behalf of the poets, he outlined how dyspepsia afflicted him, emphasizing the possibility that there were additional stomach conditions, and pointed out as well the possibly disastrous consequences of cutting mutton on the diagonal rather than longitudinally. The noble language intimidated the Scottish maids, who were already shaken by his sorcerer turn. They wondered if they might see him disappear up the chimney. At night, he'd climb out the window and the peasants on the outskirts of Edinburgh would see his mud-and-leaf-plastered shadow lurking about against the flickering light of a lantern.

He sat on the sofa next to the fireplace when he

wrote. The fire stayed lit, summer and winter. The room was snowed under with manuscripts, drafts, papers. There was a narrow path leading from the door to the fireplace and then over to the carafe. He groomed his manuscripts with a brush. This, according to James Hogg in his account of meeting De Quincey, made him an enigmatic sphinx. He wore a heavy wool cape, threadbare with holes, buttoned up to his chin; his shoes were knitted to his feet, and his pants stained black with ink. He seemed empty. They generally thought of him as an incendiary. "Papa" one of his daughters said, "your hair is on fire." De Quincey smoothed away the sparks with a hand. He was sometimes overcome with sleepiness in his studio and nodded off, pulling the candles down with him. Ash reliefs adorned his manuscripts. When the flames got too high he'd run to block the door, afraid someone would burst in and throw water on his papers. He put out fires with his robe, or the rug—the thin cleric wrapped his words in smoke, chains, links, captivity, bondage.

When invited to dinner, he promised attendance, holding forth on the subject of the enchantments of punctuality. At the appointed time, however, he was elsewhere. Perhaps he was studying pages piled up like bales of hay in one of the many shelters that he never remembered having rented. Paper storage, fragments of delirium eaten away by dust.

He married Margaret Simpson, the daughter of a salesman, and they had eight children whom he educated himself. Sara Coleridge publicly accused De Quincey of having neglected the children's education and even of having introduced them to opium. Julius died at four years old; William, the eldest boy, was taken by an obscure brain disease; and Horatio fell in China serving his country. The ascension to the throne of Queen Victoria as well as the emancipation of black slaves left him indifferent. He was distant from the terrors of the living. In a letter to Miss Mitford, De Quincey mentioned an "dark frenzy of horror" that expanded to cover everything that he was writing. Everything would be suddenly wrapped in a "sheet of consuming fire." Paper seemed poisoned to his eyes. He spent the last years of his life reworking and correcting his drafts for *Selections Grave and Gay, from Writings Published and Unpublished,* which would run fourteen volumes and be complete in 1860. On October 22, 1859, he received a visit from Mr. Begbie who found him seated on the divan, head resting perched on a pillow on a chair in front of him. He had assumed such a position, not because of the pain, but because of his extremely weak state. He could barely read through one eye and yet was scrutinizing Allibone's *Dictionary of English Literature.* In November he fell asleep in the middle of the day, from sheer fatigue, and when he woke, he looked around in surprise. It would be necessary to reassure him of the identity of the people around him and about the objects in the room. At times he discerned the "footsteps of angels" and would address himself to the deceased. Then he delighted in the supreme calm. He declared that he'd been invited to the great feast of Jesus

Christ along with the children and instructed them to dress in white from head to toe. He was then devastated when select Edinburgh miscreants saw the children dressed in white crossing Lothian Street and began to mock them, resulting in the children's great embarrassment. On Tuesday, December 6, he stayed in his chair and conversed with agility but lacked his customary ease. That day he refused food and by Wednesday morning, it seemed evident that his hours were numbered. He recognized his eldest daughter in the afternoon. "Thank you," he said simply, to whoever was around him—his tone was sweet and his expression radiant. He thought he saw his sister Elizabeth and called out to her. His breath grew slow. Then he went numb, lost consciousness gradually, and in the first hours of December 8, he died. A semblance of youth came over his face. He was seventy-four years old but seemed a boy of fourteen. They didn't allow the morning light into the room and at nine they lit the candles. His death, according to Mr. Begbie, was caused by a state of the generalized extenuation of the organism rather than by a specific illness. They said that he had been a "good sick man," and a gracious corpse; he hadn't wanted to trouble anyone. Mr. Begbie noted that he had not been affected by *senilis stultitia quae deliratio appellari solet.*

*John Keats*

In 1803, the guillotine was a common children's toy. Children also had toy cannons that fired real gunpowder, and puzzles depicting the great battles of England. They went around chanting, "Victory or death!" Do childhood games influence character? We have to assume that they do, but let's set aside such heartbreaking speculations for a moment. War—it's not even a proper game—leaves influenza in its wake, and cadavers. Do childhood games typically leave cadavers behind in the nursery? Massacres in those little fairy-dust minds? Hoist the banners of victory across the table from the marzipan mountain to the pudding! It's perhaps a dreadful thought, but we've seen clear evidence that both children and adults have a taste for imitation. Certainly, such questions should be explored, and yet let us allow that there is a purely metaphysical difference between a toy guillotine and war. Children are metaphysical creatures, a gift they lose too early, sometimes at the very moment they learn to talk.

John Keats was seven years old and in school at Enfield. He was seized by the spirit of the time, by a peculiar compulsion, an impetuous fury—before writing poetry. Any pretext seemed to him a good one for picking a fight with a friend, any pretext to fight.

Fighting was to John Keats like eating or drinking. He sought out aggressive boys, cruel boys, but their company, as he was already inclined to poetry, must have provided some comic and burlesque treats. For mere brutality—without humor, make-believe, or whimsy—didn't interest him. Which might lead a person to extrapolate that boys aren't truly brutal. Yes, they are, but they have rules and an aesthetic. Keats was a child of action. He'd punched a yard monitor more than twice his size, and he was considered a strong boy, lively and argumentative. When he was brawling, his friend Clarke reports,

Keats resembled Edmund Kean at theatrical heights
of exasperation. His friends predicted a brilliant future for him in the military. Yet when his temper de-
fused, he'd grow extremely calm, and his sweetness
shone — with the same intensity as his rage had. The
scent of angels. His earliest brushes with melancholy
were suddenly disrupted by outbursts of nervous
laughter. Moods, vague and tentative, didn't settle
over him so much as hurry past like old breezes. A
year before leaving Enfield — the Georgian-style
school building would later be converted into a train
station and then ultimately be demolished — John
Keats discovered Books. Books were the spoils left
by the Incas, by Captain Cook's voyages, *Robinson
Crusoe*. He went to battle in Lemprière's dictionary
of classical myth, among the reproductions of an-
cient sculptures and marbles, the annals of Greek fa-
ble, in the arms of goddesses. He walked through the
gardens, a book in hand. During recreation breaks,
he read Elizabethan translations of Ovid. Schol-
ars have made a habit of pointing out that the poet

didn't know Greek. *So what?* Even Lord Byron insin-
uated that Keats hadn't done anything more than set
Lemprière to verse. In the same way that the translation errors from Greek don't at all invalidate Hölder-
lin's *Der Archipelagus,* Keats's own transposed Greek
perhaps allowed him to tear up the fields of Albion
with the shards of classical ruins. He revealed to no
one that he was an orphan. The tutors were glued
to his side. He forgot his birthday and decided to
study medicine. He learned how to leech, pull teeth,
and suture. He observed cadavers on the dissection
table that had been purchased off the resurrection
men for three or four guinea each. The naked bodies
were delivered in sacks. Keats took notes and in the
margins sketched skulls, fruit, and flowers. He felt
alone. The "blue devils" settled along with him into
the damp room. He frequented the Mathew family,
his cousins, Ann and Caroline, who had a righteous
horror of the frivolities of youth.

They picked out piano arias from *Don Giovanni*
and the young men danced the quadrille. It's said

that John Keats's very first passion was for a stranger he'd seen for half an hour. He was waiting for her to smile at him but she never did. John Spurgin wanted to make a Swedenborgian of him. Keats's friend Charles Cowden Clarke procured his books. Clarke was a massively tall man with bushy hair; eight years older than Keats, he had a great interest in cricket, about which he wrote a handbook. He would also write about Chaucer and Shakespeare. Keats played cricket too.

His appearance was transformed in a single afternoon in 1813 at a lecture about Spenser. Seeming suddenly both large and potent, he emerged from his diminutive stature while reciting the verses that had struck him. He devoured books, he copied, translated sections, he became the scribe and secretary to his mind. He informed his friends at Guy's Hospital that poetry was "the only thing worth the attention of superior minds." And it would become his sole ambition. He dressed like a poet, collar turned up and tied with a black ribbon. For a short time he grew a mustache. When exam day arrived, everyone was sure that he wouldn't pass, what with those poetic airs. He did earn his diploma and would be able to work as an apothecary. But he chose to leave medicine. He was only twenty years old when he saw his own poem, "To Solitude," published in the *Examiner*.

It was impossible for his talent not to draw the attention of many people. Leigh Hunt, imprisoned for having libeled the king, protected Keats as long as Keats let him. John Hamilton Reynolds thought of him as a brother. Severn perceived ecstasy in his face and about his features—but then, Severn was a painter. He observed that his head was too small for his broad shoulders, observed the intensity of his gaze that blazed like a flame when crossed but when calm glittered like a lake at dusk, and noted a cold lethargy. They visited museums together. He saw Brown, Dilke, Bailey, Hazlitt. Things were lukewarm with Shelley. Haydon showed him the Elgin Marbles from the Parthenon. Keats didn't have the money to travel the world but made a long walking tour of Scotland. He wore a sack on his back filled with old clothes and new socks, pens, paper, ink, Cary's translation of the *Divine Comedy,* and a draft of *Isabella.* His traveling companion was the clerk and writer Charles Armitage Brown, a practical and energetic man. Keats returned home ragged and feverish, his jacket torn and his shoes missing, but he had scaled a mountain, the Ben Nevis. He was poor, according to W. B. Yeats, and couldn't build a Gothic castle as Beckford had, which inclined him instead toward the pleasures of the imagination. Yeats also said that Keats was malnourished, of weak health, and had no family. But aren't all poets the heralds of Heaven?

According to the testimony of friends, Keats was of small stature, though rather muscular, with a broad chest and broad shoulders (almost too broad); his legs were underdeveloped in proportion to his torso. He gave off the impression of strength. His chestnut hair was abundant and fine.

He parted it with a ruler and it fell across his face in heavy silken curls. He had a high, rather sloped, forehead. His nose was beautiful but his mouth— they were specific on this point—was big and not intellectual. His lower lip was pronounced, giving him a combative aspect, which diminished his elegance a bit, yet served, they were quick to add, to animate his physiognomy. His face was oval and there was something feminine about his wide forehead and pointy chin. Despite his disproportionate mouth, Keats, they'd concede, was handsome. Sometimes he had the look in his eyes of a Delphic priestess on the hunt for visions.

According to Haydon, he was the only one who knew him—with the sole exception of Wordsworth, who'd predicted great acclaim for him based on his looks.

He was brilliant socially, loved wordplay, and his eruptions of laughter were noisy and extended. People found him irresistibly funny when he did impressions. If he didn't like the conversation, he'd retreat to a window corner and look out into the void. His friends respected that corner as if it were his by law.

If a face, as Johann Gottfried Herder says, is nothing more than a *Spiegelkammer* of the spirit, then we should be a little frightened of Keats's variety of expressions. Even doubt insinuates itself. When Keats wrote, "I thought a lot about Poetry," we can't see in that a mirror reflection of Keats. The mirror is empty, uninhabited. The idea has no facial features and could look like anything, but theologically it's *more beautiful* empty. Keats is unable to contemplate himself. His gift is not knowing how to reconcile himself. The identity of a person who is in the room with him presses in and cancels his own out in a flash. When Keats speaks, he's not sure that he's the one talking. When he dreamed of bobbing in the turbine in Canto V of Dante's *Inferno*, it was one of the great joys of his life.

Joseph Severn's portrait is described by some as a lie drawn from truth: friends found it too effeminate, the trembling mouth, and yet the eyes were right, even radiant. The painting's three-quarter view makes the eyes seem even bigger, more remarkable. His focus rests above the earth yet not in the sky—fixed on a murky horizon. His pupils are slightly enlarged, trained perpendicularly on the suspended thought. Even his gaze is indolent, sensual, consciously engrossed, and like a veil shifting across his brow, there is a flash of charming zealotry. He looks like a girl, and if we think of him as a girl, the femininity of his features evaporates and he seems stubborn and volatile, the constant surveyor of his own visions.

One day in Haydon's study, Keats recited "Hymn to Pan." Wordsworth was there; he kept his left hand tucked into his waistcoat. "With reverence" was the way he'd inscribed a book of his poems for Keats and he was truly reverent about poetry. Wordsworth's wife was once heard to say, "Mr. Wordsworth is never interrupted." Keats dared open his mouth anyway. He recited his verse in that singsong way of his while pacing up and down the room. In the space between his voice and the paintings on the wall there was a plastic silence. "A very pretty piece of paganism," said Wordsworth, his left hand still tucked into his waistcoat. Haydon was distressed by Wordsworth's utter tactlessness and angered by his use of the word "paganism." And yet we read in Meister Eckhart that through their virtue, the pagan masters had ascended higher even than Saint Paul, and that experience was what had brought them as high as the apostles had come through grace.

There were women Keats didn't dislike. Miss Cox, an Anglo-Indian heiress, had a theatrical Asian beauty and was therefore despised by the Reynolds sisters. She kept him awake one night the way a Mozart piece might. "I speak of the thing as a passtime and an amuzement than which I can feel none deeper than a conversation with an imperial woman the very 'yes' and 'no' of whose Lips is to me a Banquet."

Isabella Jones was a few years older than Keats

and had read "Endymion." They met when she was staying with an elderly Irish relative in the village of Bo Peep near Hastings. Biographers have questions about her—the two took walks, took tea together in the garden, and played whist late into the night—was this a summer fling or an initiation? The prevailing view is that it was an initiation.

What took the form of a young woman who'd moved in nearby was almost a matter of sorcery. For some time, Keats didn't want anyone to utter her name. Her mere existence was secret. Fanny Brawne was descended from knights, monks, and lawyers. Her mother had married for love against her parents' wishes—like Keats's own mother who'd married the stable boy at the Swan and Hoop Inn. Fanny acquired Beau Brummell as a cousin when her mother's sister married. From her paternal ancestors who'd performed at the Garrick, Fanny inherited a proclivity for the theater. Grandfather Brawne had supported the liberation of women. It was said about Fanny that she wasn't very beautiful, but undoubtedly elegant. Her nostrils were too thin, her face too long, the nose aquiline, and her pallor chronic. Her cheeks were never rosy, not even after a six-mile walk. The history of female beauty is almost always told in the negative. Even the Brontë sisters were talked about as plain, as was Emily Dickinson. Spiritual sex appeal does not seem to generate chivalry. Fanny was the same height as Keats, just over five feet tall. His nickname for her was "Millimant." From the moment she met him, Fanny was taken with his conversation. Generally, she found men to be fools. Was compelled to describe herself as "not timid or modest in the least." She conversed in French with the émigrés at the Hampstead "colony." She danced with officers at the St. John's Wood barracks. She had an eighteenth-century way about her, her hair curled in the style of the court of Charles II. Fanny had a "fire in her heart." Her mother made inquiries about Keats with the neighbors. They were engaged. Keats signed his letters to her with the emblem of a Greek lyre with four broken strings and the motto: *Qui me néglige me désole.* Walking on the heath, Keats came across a being with a strange light in its eyes, a rumpled archangel—he recognized Coleridge. They walked together and spoke of nightingales and dreams.

"That drop of blood is my death-warrant. I must die," pronounced Keats calmly on the third of February 1820. He seemed intoxicated. His future was not predicted by a Sibyl, but by the medical student himself, the poet whose verses describe beauty flooded by a mortal estuary. With the intensity he'd once applied to his anatomy studies, he scrutinized the blood on his handkerchief. He felt like he was suffocating and only managed to fall asleep after hours of despotic insomnia. On the third day he was well enough to receive visitors and read news of George III's death. Doctor Rodd came to see him. His lungs were not compromised but the doctor recommended mental rest. They determined that the hemorrhage was simply the body trying to fight off the recent bout of cholera that his brother George had suffered. They soothed him with currant jellies and compotes, some of which dripped onto a Ben Jonson first edition. This extreme diet provoked strong palpitations. Doctor Bree, a specialist, was summoned. They could find no ailments in his lungs or other organic causes. Keats's illness "is in his head," they concluded. For a day, he was tormented by Fanny's specter, which appeared to him dressed as a shepherdess and then in a ball gown. She was a joyful simulacrum dancing and giggling in the void.

The morning of June 22, he had light bleeding. In the afternoon he went to the Hunts for tea. They talked about an Italian tenor. There was a lady there who was particularly interested in bel canto and was amazed that the young gentleman was the author of "Endymion." The bleeding got worse over the course of the evening. He spends the twenty-third laid out in a room, far from Fanny, staring at flowers on a table. Speech is difficult. He indicates the verses he favors in a volume of Spenser he wants to give to Fanny. The doctor Darling prescribes a trip to Italy. Keats's hands are like those of an old man, veins swollen; his features, Severn reports, have taken on the same cast his brother Tom's did when he was dying of consumption. The evanescent hand furiously traced an oblique line over the first copy of his book. In a preface, the publisher apologized for the unfinished "Hyperion." It is the first of July. There is a metal taste in his mouth. "If I die," he tells Brown, "you must ruin Lockhart." For he was the one who'd written an insulting article about Keats that touted gossip and personal details. Unsigned—yet Keats applied his sleuthing talents and located an inside source to identify that enemy of literature.

Keats considered going just anywhere in order to die alone. Then he wanted Brown to go with him. But he was to leave for Rome with Severn. On the twentieth of August he started coughing blood again. His friends began to say their farewells. Fare-

wells to dying people are often awkward. Haydon
started off the ceremony. By way of comfort, he began to speak about life after death—the last thing
that Keats wanted to hear. Angered, Keats answered
that if he didn't get better right away he'd rather
kill himself. John Hamilton Reynolds was unable
to take his hand. He wrote to John Taylor that he
was happy about Keats's departure, that he *should*
be running from Leigh Hunt's vain and cruel company. As for Fanny, Keats only benefited from the
absence of the poor thing—to whom he was so
incomprehensibly bound. Fanny wrote in her di-
ary: "Mr. Keats leaves Hampstead." Keats gave her
the Severn miniature, a copy of Dante, a copy of
Spenser, and his Shakespeare folio. They exchanged
locks of hair and rings. Fanny sewed a silk lining
into his traveling hat and also gave him a journal
and a knife. Woodhouse also took a lock of his
hair. He wanted to be Keats's Boswell. The *Maria
Crowther* set sail. It was a small two-rigger and when
the sea got rough it disappeared beneath the waves.

It had one cabin intended for six people. There was
the Captain, a good man; Lady Pidgeon, plump
and pleasant; and Mistress Cotterell who was gracious though in an advanced state of consumption.
But then there was a typhoid epidemic in London,
the ship was quarantined, and it was October 31
by the time that ended and Keats was twenty-five
years old. When Mistress Cotterell disembarked
in Naples she asked, a little too loudly, after the
moribund youth. They arrived in Rome on the fif-
teenth of November. Doctor Clark was waiting for
them. His bedside manner had been acclaimed by
the King of Belgium and Queen Victoria. He was
a Scot. While attending Keats, he had only minor
concerns about what was afflicting the heart and
lungs and said that the more serious trouble was
in his stomach. Mental exertions were the source
of the trouble. The doctor recommended fresh air
and moderate exercise. He had Keats throw all his
medicines to the dogs. He suggested horseback rid-
ing and rented a horse for him at six pounds ster-

ling a month. The landlady, Anna Angeletti, asked
five pounds sterling in rent. Keats desired a piano
and so that was rented as well. Doctor Clark lent
him several pieces of music, throwing in a Haydn
sonata as well. The food was fetid. On one occasion, Keats threw it out the window after tasting it.
Shortly thereafter he was brought an excellent meal.

He started reading Alfieri's *Tragedie* but had to
stop after the first few pages—not being able to con-
tain his emotions. He wrote a last letter to Brown,
attempting an awkward bow and a grand farewell.
On the tenth of December after vomiting blood,
he asked Severn for laudanum. The attacks over
the next week were violent. He suffered from hunger. Clark rationed his food severely because of the
ruined state of Keats's digestive apparatus; one an-
chovy on toast a day. Keats begged for more food.
He couldn't sleep. He suspected that someone back
in London had poisoned him. The servants didn't
dare come into his room because they feared he was
contagious. On Christmas Day, Severn perceived in

his friend's desperation that Keats was "dying in horror." As a good Christian, Severn tried to convince
Keats that there was redemption in pain. Keats dictated a list of books that he wanted to read: Bun-
yan's *Pilgrim's Progress*, Jeremy Taylor's *Holy Living
and Holy Dying*, and Madame Dacier's translation of
Plato. Three letters arrived that day. The letter from
Fanny remained unopened. At the end of December the landlady reported Keats's illness to the police. Severn didn't go out to sketch ruins but stayed
at Keats's side instead. Keats was overcome by sleep
and Severn drew a portrait of Keats's head on his pillow, eyes closed, face hollowed, a few curls glued
to his forehead with cold sweat. Then transcribed
Keats's words, his last testimony. Severn was in the
presence of a great poet. He may have been already
thinking that one day he would be buried beside
him. He'd been to visit the Protestant cemetery near
the Pyramid of Cestius, its grounds were glazed
over with violets and it seemed that Keats liked the
spot. He said he would feel the flowers grow over

him. Severn knew that violets were Keats's favorite flower. He plucked for him a just budded rose, a winter rose. Keats received it darkly and said "I hope to no longer be alive in spring." He wanted what he called in his last letter a "posthumous existence" to come to an end. Inscribed on his gravestone: "Here lies one whose name was writ in water." His words are set into the stone as if on a mirror, touching everything and not touched by anything—strange asymmetry.

Stretched out on his bed, he gazed up at the rose pattern in the blue ceiling tiles. His eyes grew glassy. He spoke for hours in a lucid delirium. He never lost his faculties. He prepared Severn for his death. He wondered whether he'd ever seen anyone die before. He worried about the complications that might come up. He consoled Severn and told him that it wouldn't last long and that he wouldn't have convulsions. He longed for death with frightening urgency. On the twenty-third of February he worried about his friend Severn's breathing, how it pressed on him like ice. He tried again to reassure him: "It will be easy." Dusk entered the room. From when Keats said that he was about to die, seven hours passed. His breath stopped. Death animated him in the last moment. After the autopsy, Clark said that he couldn't understand how Keats had survived so long. Fanny's last letters, never read by anyone, were sealed in his coffin. After the funeral service, the police took possession of the apartment on Piazza Spagna. They stripped the walls and floor and burned all of the furniture.

*Marcel Schwob*

Mayer André Marcel Schwob was born into a family of doctors and rabbis. His mother, Mathilde, was a Cahun, descended from Caym of Sainte-Menehould who had followed Joinville across the sea during the Crusades and, it is said, nursed him to health when he fell sick with cholera at Acre. From his maternal great-grandfather, Anselme, the rabbi of Hachfelden, Schwob had inherited an ample forehead, sensual mouth, and a sad half smile in his eyes. Marcel was proud of his lineage yet often preferred not to frequent people of his lineage. His head was stuffed with names, words, and legends. By the time he was three he spoke French, German, and English. The house on Rue de l'Église in Chaville was a silent house. His mother climbed the stairs on tiptoe. Even when the Prussians stole wine from the cellar

they took great care around the delicate child—he
was too precocious, too intelligent, and he suffered
from a brain fever. Over the course of his illness he
was confined to bed in a shuttered room. During
this time he went on many long voyages. Slightly
afflicted by rickets, he dreamed of swimming across
the English Channel. Upon arrival, he fell into the
arms of Jules Verne. He was also friendly with Edgar Allan Poe, with whom he visited once he had
chased away the German tutor. He set up his night
table to accommodate his visitors. When he was
with Edgar and Jules, he was surrounded by conversation, which made him then abhor children of his
own age with all their infantile wheezing. His ab-
sorption in these dialogues was such that he had no
awareness of the hours passing, or even the years.
Suddenly he was fifteen years old and devouring
Auguste Brachet's *Grammaire comparée*. His uncle,
Léon Cahun, author of *La vie juive*, became his tutor and mentor. After all, who was better suited to

mentor Schwob than a Cahun? The same Cahun who was a curator at the Bibliothèque Mazarine. Léon told stories about adventurers, sailors, and soldiers. He had traveled through Asia Minor and along the Euphrates. He was very knowledgeable and even spoke Uyghur.

Marcel met a strange melancholy boy at school, Georges Guieysse. The two quickly became inseparable and began working together. Every page Marcel wrote passed through Georges's hands. They were like Renaissance Humanists: Marcel composed letters to him in Greek and signed off in Arabic—or sometimes just with a simple "*shake hands*." Marcel confided in Georges: he was often incredibly tired, his ideas escaped, his memory got fragmented. Why not go to Australia or Canada and become kitchen boys. And then Georges wasn't around for a period. When they did see each other, Georges would crouch in the corner, clasping at his spleen, while his scholarly friend went on, building itineraries for the voyages they would one day take. On the seventh of May 1889, Georges Guieysse shot himself through the heart. He was twenty years old.

From that point on, Marcel took up residence in the severe, often deserted halls and archives of the Bibliothèque Mazarine where he unearthed papers about François Villon and the band of Coquillards. He turned into a writer. One evening in autumn, when the rain was already cold, he met a young working girl with a childish spirit and fell in love. Louise is skinny, consumed by tuberculosis, just a wretch with brown hair, her almond eyes dazed and scornful. She writes him notes in colored pencil. Marcel is enchanted by the foolish little things Louise tells him. An example: "Pookie, my hair is falling out, don't forget how your nails grow and the scales from your skin fall. My tummy hurts. I sewed up my doll's nose and now it's much shorter and fatter. But I forgot to leave her nostrils. I'll have to go back in with the scissors later but for now I seem to have lost them. Don't forget to bring me a new pair when you come. At least then you'll be helpful. Pookiewooky."

A passion for play overtook the wise man. His pockets were always full of cotton string, needles, and fabric squares with colored borders. He smiled a lot and spoke in a falsetto voice with the publisher of the newspaper, a man he hated. In the meantime, Marcel was apprehensively watching over Baby Vise's condition. The doctors were aghast by the unhygienic conditions in which she lived: such a tiny room, not a whiff of air, the window was only a few centimeters wide and always kept closed. Louise smoked one cigarette after another, or cigars, or Marcel's pipe, and she drank coffee. Louise died before long. After the funeral the unhappy writer returned to the room; he arranged all of the babies in a trunk and brought them home. His friends stayed with him at all times, because whenever he was left alone, Marcel got frightened that the dead girl would die again. He sees her ghost laughing in the corners of the room; its watery eyes seem to suggest

new games. Marcel packs the scissors and pocket-
knives into a box, and he throws away the needles
and the scraps. He grows superstitious and always
wants to sleep. Even in his sleep he can hear echoes
of her coarse laughter, but he can no longer hear the
chirping and nonsense in her—the child aged in
death. When he looks at himself in the mirror the
next morning he has grown old—his hair has fallen
out overnight, and now his forehead is even larger.

He started using morphine. It provided mo-
ments of great solitude. When his friends leave,
he bolts his doors and windows after them so that
not a sound filters through—perennial hours strat-
ify like eternity across the room. This is when he
became the true Great Sheik of Knowledge and
Grimoires, which was the honorific Doctor Jean-
Claude Mardrus bestowed on him in his dedication
to volume XV of his translation of *Le livre des mille
nuits et une nuit*. Mardrus had a honeyed voice and
his laughter on occasion irritated Schwob. He wore
long capes with embroidered edges and pendant

buttons, the inside pockets heavy with gold coins. The extraordinary legends Mardrus told were interpolated with stories of money. Before too long, Schwob preferred to do away with that friendship too. He conceived of writing the *Vies imaginaires.* Those men who live like dogs, those sainted women credulous in the face of any clever monk, those who damn themselves, indulging a longing for everything beneath them—this was the company that Schwob kept now. He realizes that he's smiling when he reads his own words aloud to himself. "Don't embrace the dead because they suffocate the living ... Don't go into cemeteries. The dead are pestilent." Schwob was already sick and he knew he'd never recover.

He married the actress Marguerite Moreno in 1900 in London. That same year, in a pavilion at the Exposition Universelle in Paris, Marcel met a young Chinese man named Ting, and hired him as a manservant. He decided to follow in the footsteps of Robert Louis Stevenson, "55 percent artist and 45 percent adventurer," with whom he'd cultivated a long correspondence. Schwob and Ting set off for the South Seas on board the *Ville de La Ciotat*. Upon learning of the departure, Schwob's friend Jules Renard quipped, "He lives his stories before dying." On the boat there were corrupt functionaries, colonial magistrates who never stopped talking, a civilian family with four bullish daughters with thick red braids, and an albino boy who looked like a fat farm girl wearing men's clothes. Right away, the voyage seemed too long. In Colombo he drowsily contemplated the babel of religion. There were cartloads of people praying in a cavern, a Tamil feast. He was always tired and it was hard to breathe; the hot wind blew at him and dust and flies stuck to his skin. The Australian landscape seemed sinister, long cadaverous beaches where the brush moved in the wind like the gnarled hair of dead people. In Samoa they called him *Tulapla,* the talk man, and kept him up late into the night telling stories. He shook the hand of King Mataafa, who looked like Bismarck. Schwob did not get to Stevenson's tomb under the flowers on top of Mount Vaea. He didn't find what he was looking for. A certain Captain Crawshaw showed him some notes in Stevenson's hand—one of them recommended mystery and discretion and also begged Crawshaw to locate Captain Wurmbrand in Tonga and bring him back. Wurmbrand was an Austrian adventurer of whom Stevenson was very fond. It was a nuanced wandering through memories, leading toward the enchanted shadows. A crumpled catalog remains from his long journey. He met tearful imposters who dragged themselves before him with business propositions, ruined con men, the ragtag mobs of brigands and criminals that he knew so well. In the midst of that busy soup he yearned for his room in Paris.

Upon returning there, he shut himself into his house so that he could breathe. The titles of books he would never write: *Océanide, Vaililoa, Captain Crabbe.* He would never again want to leave. He felt like a "dog cut open alive." Won't the dead come to talk for just half an hour with this sick man? His face colored slightly, turning into a mask of gold. His eyes stayed open imperiously. No one could close his eyelids. The room smoked of grief.